Library of Congress Cataloging-in-Publication Data is available.
A CIP catalogue record for this book is available from The British Library.

ISBN-13: 978-0-7358-2130-9 / ISBN-10: 0-7358-2130-5 (trade edition)

10 9 8 7 6 5 4 3 2 1

Printed in Slovakia

Index to Paintings

1. Unknown (ca.1279–1255 B.C.E.): *Portrait of Queen Nefertiti*

2. Leonardo da Vinci (1452–1519): *Mona Lisa*, ca. 1503, Paris, Musée du Louvre

3. Rembrandt van Rijn (1606–1669): *Self-Portrait at the Easel*, 1660, Paris, Musée du Louvre

4. Claude Monet (1840–1926): *Nympheas at Night*, 1897–1898, Paris, Musée Marmottan

5. Vincent van Gogh (1853–1890): *Self-Portrait with Grey Hat*, Amsterdam, Rijksmuseum Vincent van Gogh

6. Paul Gauguin (1848–1903): *Women of Tahiti on the Beach*, 1891, Paris, Musée d'Orsay

7. Edvard Munch (1863–1944): *The Scream*, 1893, Oslo, Munch-Museet © the Munch Museum / The Munch Ellingsen Group / VG Bild-Kunst, Bonn 2004

8. Paul Klee (1879–1940): *Legend of the Nile*, 1937, 215 (U 15), 69 x 61 cm. Pastel on cotton jute. Paste color on wedge frame, frame strips. Condition of preservation: the original frame strips have not been preserved (1993). Kunstmuseum Bern, Hermann and Margrit Rupf-Stiftung. © VG Bild-Kunst, Bonn 2004

9. Wassily Kandinsky (1866–1944): *Sky-blue*, 1940, Paris, Musée National d'Art Moderne. © VG Bild-Kunst, Bonn 2004

10. Henri Matisse (1869–1954): *Icarus* © Succession H. Matisse / VG Bild-Kunst, Bonn 2004

11. Mark Rothko (1903–1970): *Orange and Yellow* © Kate Rothko-Prizel & Christopher Rothko / VG Bild-Kunst, Bonn 2004

12. Juan Gris (1887–1927): *Harlequin with Guitar*, 1919, Sammlung Kahnweiler; Paris, Musée d'Art Moderne

13. Salvador Dalí (1904–1989): *The Persistence of Memory*, 1931, New York, Museum of Modern Art, © Salvador Dalí, Foundation Gala-Salvador Dalí / VG Bild-Kunst, Bonn 2004

14. Niki de Saint Phalle (1930–2002): *Nana*, Hannover-Langenhagen. Photo: J. Schian, Hannover, www.schian-hannover.de

15. Andy Warhol (1928–1987): *Che Guevara*, Montage (1962?). This painting by Gerard Malanga, in the style of Andy Warhol's Marilyn Monroe pictures, was based on a photograph by Jim Fitzpatrick. Warhol actually never created this painting, but he authenticated it in return for all the profits.

16. Keith Haring (1958–1990): *Untitled*, 1984 © The Estate of Keith Haring, New York

Archiv für Kunst und Geschichte, Berlin: 2, 3, 5, 6, 7, 12, 13
Bilderarchive Preußischer Kulturbesitz, Berlin: 10
The Bridgeman Art Library, Berlin: 8, 9
Jürgen Schian, Hannover: 14

Henri, Egg Artiste

By Marcus Pfister

Translated by J. Alison James

NorthSouth
BOOKS
New York / London

Henri and Henrietta lived in a cottage tucked away behind a thicket of bushes, right beside a large cornfield. It was a perfect place for rabbits because, if danger threatened, they could simply hide in the high corn. Next to the cottage they had a small barn where Henri worked. Everything was quite cozy.

Henri was a professional Easter egg painter. Henrietta helped bring fresh eggs into the barn.

Easter was coming soon, and Henrietta had already been gathering eggs for some time. Normally, Henri would start to paint them straight away. But when Henrietta brought in the last eggs, Henri still hadn't lifted a finger.

"Henri!" she said reproachfully. "Don't you need to get to work? Easter is right around the corner!"

"Oh, enough with the eggs!" snapped Henri. "I'm sick of them. I will never paint Easter eggs again. This is not a barn, it's my art studio!" Henri said. "I'm an artist—not a farmer!"

"I beg your pardon?" asked Henrietta. She couldn't believe her long ears. "Surely you can't mean that! Oh, Henri, think of all the children who are waiting for your Easter eggs. You can't disappoint them!"

"The children? I'm sure they're sick of eggs, too. Same old painted eggs, year after year."

"Think about last Easter, Henri. Your eggs were so wonderful."

"Yes, they were lovely. Just as lovely as they were the year before that. And the year before that. And exactly as lovely as they were three years ago. They were always lovely, and they were always exactly the same. I've had enough!" said Henri, and he stormed outside.

"Why don't you dye them with grass and herbs and onionskins?" suggested Henrietta. "You got all those wonderful brown and gold and ocher tints when you did that before."

"Oh, like that hasn't been done before," snapped Henri. "Last time, I was up to my neck in stinky old onionskins. I don't need that again. I am an artiste! I need new ideas! And above all, I need my PEACE AND QUIET!" With that, he disappeared into his studio and slammed the door shut.

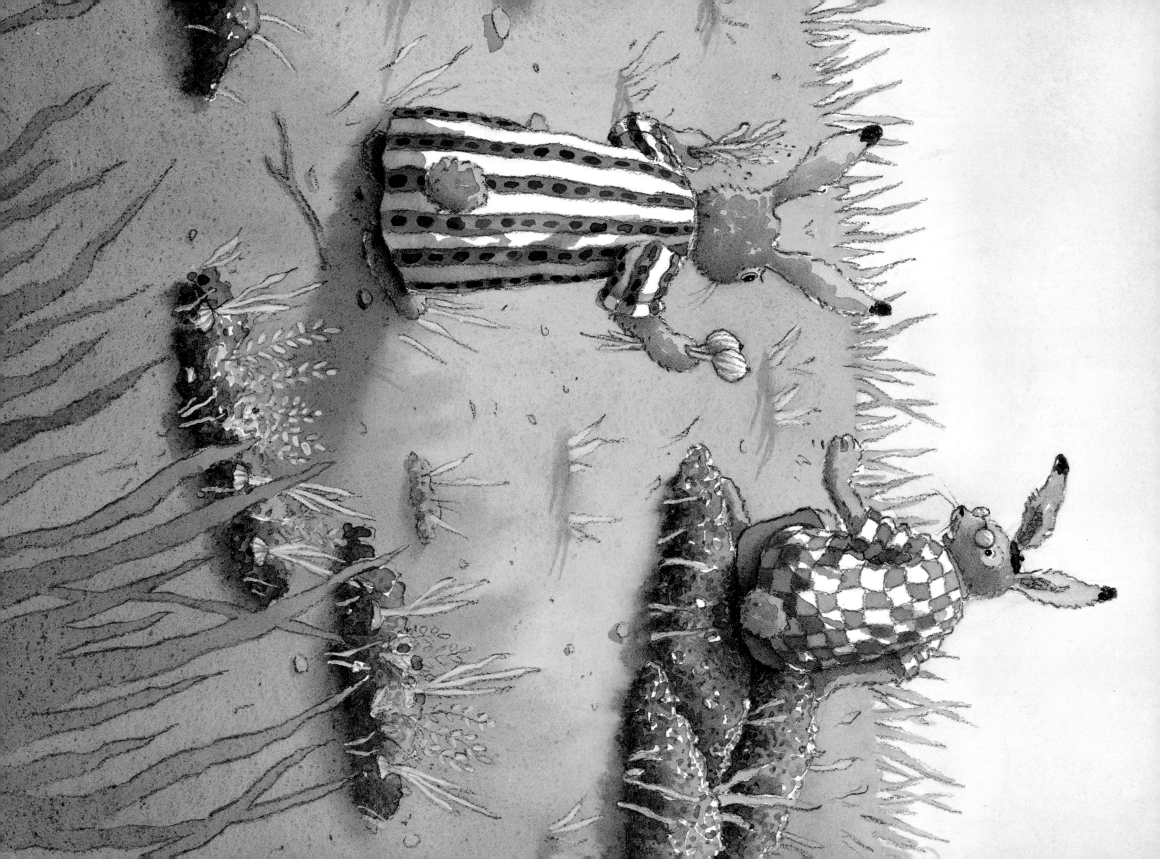

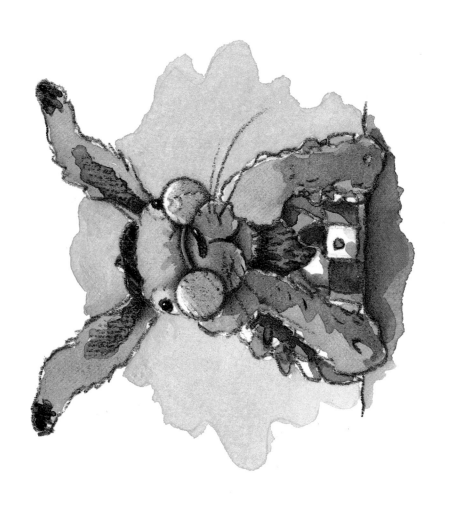

Cranky as he was, of course Henri knew that the eggs had to be painted. When it came down to it, the truth was that he, Henri, was quite famous for his eggs. Even so, he was determined that this year his eggs would look different. Quite different.

At last, inspiration struck. He would create artistic masterpieces! Artwork that the world had never seen before! Henri carefully settled an egg on the easel and began to paint. He worked all night.

When Henrietta nervously poked her nose through the door the next morning, she saw the first finished egg. It was a painting of a hare, in blocks and layers of bold blue, red, and brown. It was hard even to recognize the figure. Henrietta didn't know what to say.

"Uh, Henri, don't you think you can do better than that? The funny hat, the red eye—it doesn't look like something children would enjoy." Henri glared at Henrietta and pointed silently at the door.

By that evening his second work was completed. Henri had painted a female rabbit, but it, too, was unusual. Henri's best friend, Marty Mole, gaped in astonishment when he peeked through the window. What was that rabbit wearing on its head?

Bewildered, Marty stared at the new painting. It looked as if it were from ancient Egypt!

"Children aren't going to like that, Henri," he said.

But Henri didn't listen. Carefully, he painted on the Egyptian hieroglyphics that he had been practicing.

Next, Henri painted a beautiful portrait of a lady. Secretly he wished that Henrietta and Marty would have something nice to say about it. And they did. They really liked this new painting.

"Wonderful," said Henrietta. "That looks just like one of the mothers from last year."

Henri nodded and was proud that Henrietta had recognized the woman.

Henri painted one egg after another without stopping. He painted with fine brushstrokes and bold, he painted bright pictures and dark, happy subjects and sad. Some paintings you could tell what they were, while others were just a dance of tints and hues.

Watching Henri at work inspired Marty to paint, too. He grabbed a brush and a sheet of paper and got to work. Henrietta didn't like all the pictures on the eggs. But she was happy that Henri had managed to finish before Easter. "Well done," she praised her exhausted husband. "Now we just need to hide the eggs and then you can have yourself a proper rest."

"Hide the eggs? Are you crazy?" Henri blazed. "Do you think I've worked day and night on these just to hide them? I'll have an exhibition, so everyone can come and appreciate them."

"I don't know, Henri. This is Easter. Children want to run around finding eggs. They aren't going to stand and look at paintings that they might not understand."

But Henri insisted. So Henrietta, Henri, Henri, and Marty set about building beautiful pedestals for the eggs. They built mounds of pebbles, padded them with fresh leaves, and then carefully set an egg on each, or searched for mossy nests on tree stumps. Egg after egg found its place in the sun. And by morning the exhibit was ready.

Although they were dead tired, they didn't want to miss the reaction of the first child hunting for Easter eggs and finding an art show instead.

The sun had dried the last drops of dew from the grass when a small girl came up the garden steps. She rubbed her eyes and stared in disbelief. Then she knelt down by one of the eggs and gazed in wonder at it.

Henrietta pulled Henri's arm and whispered, "Look, Henri—she likes it. I think your exhibit is a success after all!"